Fish for Supper

FISH FOR SUPPER

M. B. Goffstein

The New York Review Children's Collection
New York

This is a New York Review Book
Published by the New York Review of Books
435 Hudson Street, New York, NY 10014
www.nyrb.com

Library of Congress Cataloging-in-Publication Data
Names: Goffstein, M. B., author, illustrator.
Title: Fish for supper / by M. B. Goffstein.
Description: New York : New York Review Books, 2021. |
    Series: New York Review children's collection | Originally
    published in New York by Dial Press in 1976. | Summary:
    Describes Grandmother's typical day of fishing.
Identifiers: LCCN 2020012195 | ISBN 9781681375465 (hardcover)
Subjects: CYAC: Grandmothers—Fiction. | Fishing—Fiction.
Classification: LCC PZ7.G5573 Fi 2021 | DDC [E]—dc23
LC record available at https://lccn.loc.gov/2020012195

ISBN: 978-1-68137-546-5

Printed in the United States of America on acid-free paper.
10 9 8 7 6 5 4 3 2 1

To the Goffsteins

When my grandmother went fishing,

she would get up at five o'clock
in the morning

and make herself breakfast,

then clean up the dishes fast, fast,

and go down to the water
wearing her big sun hat.

With cans of worms and minnows,
some fruit for lunch,
bobbers, lines, hooks, and sinkers,

she rowed out in the rowboat

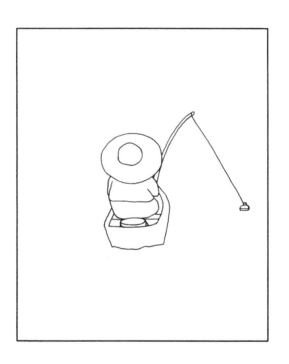

and stayed on the lake all day.

Over its sunlit waves and ripplets
she could see her yellow boathouse

staring back at her with dark eyes
from the shore,

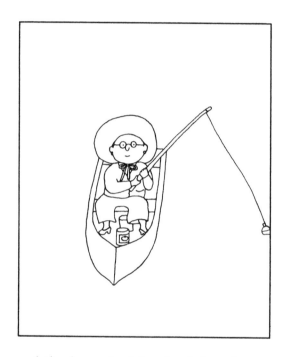

while she waited for the fish to bite.

She caught sunfish, crappies, perch,
and sometimes a big northern pike.

When she came home in the evening,

she cleaned the fish

and fried them in butter.

She took fresh rolls out of the oven,
put water for tea on the stove,

and sat down and ate very slowly,

taking care not to choke on a bone.

Then fast, fast, she cleaned up the dishes

and went to bed,

so she could get up at five o'clock
in the morning

to go fishing.

ABOUT THE AUTHOR-ARTIST

M.B. Goffstein was born in St. Paul, Minnesota in 1940. She graduated from Bennington College and moved to New York City where she began writing and illustrating books for children and adults beginning with *The Gats!* (1966) and ending with *A House, A Home* (1989). She died in 2017 having spent her last decades writing fiction, painting, and photographing objects that delighted her.